Tom F(

SWELL

www.tomforeman.co.uk

Foreword

Climate change seems to be condemned to a perpetual blind spot in the mind of British politics. We're all aware it's happening. We all know it urgently needs addressing. And yet year after year, summit after summit, promises fall short and the cries of warning continue to echo.

I think that part of the reason for this unfortunate helter-skelter towards 3°-4° of warming is that for the most part, Britain has enjoyed the effects of climate change to some level. Hotter summers and nicer English wine – it's all very easy to cheekily indulge in because after all, what can little old us do about it? The effects of climate change – you know, the *real* effects, not like here – are concentrated in an abstract and faraway global south, and the horrors are, well, horrific, but they're not happening here. Not yet. Right?

So, Swell.

It was in the midst of the first lockdown that I came across a Guardian article about a small village in Wales called Fairbourne. In 2014, the residents found out via a showing of *Week In Week out* on the BBC that their town had been earmarked by the local council as indefensible against rising sea levels, and as a result was set to be decommissioned in the next few decades. Every streetlamp, shop and sewer would be demolished and returned to a tidal salt marsh to protect against inland flooding. Property prices dropped overnight, insurance disappeared, and the residents were abandoned, unable to claim compensation or seemingly get any answers.

I was shocked it had taken me over a year from its initial publication to find this story. This was a bright flashing beacon clearly demonstrating the effect of climate change already being felt on our shores, and yet it had slipped under the radar somehow. It was hard to focus on anything much other than Covid during that time, but this made me angry, and I was instantly drawn to explore it deeper despite all the other noise.

For me, it was the human story that struck a nerve. Villages and towns are not just bricks and mortar, they're homes. They're places people have spent their whole lives, raised families, loved and lost, and

Fairbourne is surely no different. How then could it be fair to abandon the residents in such a way, with such poor communication and subsequent support?

And what makes it so devastating is that Fairbourne is likely just the first. Despite not being officially condemned, Happisburgh in Norfolk continues to literally fall into the sea as each year passes. The same is happening in Withernsea and Hornsea in Yorkshire. These 'managed retreats' will only become more common, and if they are dealt with in the same way Fairbourne has to date, we will have a very real issue of climate refugees from our own shores, let alone the refugees that the rest of the world will produce. This story needs to be told and it needs to be heard.

I try very hard in Swell to focus the story on the community, and specifically on a small host of characters led by siblings Ava and Josh. I wanted to explore how relational ties are put under strain during times of crisis, especially communal ones, as this is essentially a microcosm for what could be coming nationally down the line. So whilst the story is on the backdrop of environmental disaster, my hope is that the real essence of it is in its humanity.

It's become quite a personal story in writing it and I've really fallen deeply in love with Swell. My father's side of the family are from Whitstable in Kent, with a father-son lineage of oyster fishermen dating well back in to the 1600s (my own grandfather broke this tradition because of seasickness, would you believe). I wasn't expecting to but in telling this story I found myself feeling connected to that part of my history, which added even more layers for me in the narrative. Arthur and Dawn for example are my father's parents, and it's no accident that they share names with two of the wider characters in the play.

I invite you to explore the beautiful, tragic town of Swell, and hope that you enjoy it in whatever way you can. I really do hope that in adding my own voice to this conversation, I am helping to fight for the recognition of climate change for what it is.

Swell was first performed at Underbelly Cowgate as part of the Edinburgh Festival Fringe, premiering on August 4th, 2022, with the following cast and crew:

AVA	Rachel Nicholson
JOSH	Max Beken
ADI	Karan Maini
CREATED BY	Tom Foreman
CO-DIRECTOR	Pip Pearce
AS. PRODUCER	Tavy Oursin
TECHNICAL DIRECTOR	Tom Chandler

For Kate

SWELL

Prologue

AVA   You need to go.

JOSH   What?

AVA   You need to go, now.

JOSH   Go where?

AVA   I don't know, Josh, I don't want to know because if I know I'll have to tell them, but you need to get your shit together, right now, and get out of Swell. I'll keep quiet until the morning and then I have to tell them what I know.

JOSH   Ava, please. I swear I can make this right –

AVA   Go!

Act One

AVA   Orange streaks against red. Purple turns to blue. Bubbles froth in the pebbled cracks of the shore as the tide pulls in, in, in, and out. Down on the front in the soft morning light is where the world slows for just a second. The gulls glide. The streetlamps flicker off. The sunrises through the ocean. In these eternal seconds you feel the impossible draw of this endless plain before you. Pulling in, in, in as it has forever, and will continue always. And you feel safe in this unbreakable dance.

The town of Swell - and its 2000 sleeping residents – sits nestled between two cliff forms like the pearl of an oyster, secluded by 15 miles of jagged coastline. The day slowly wakes. The fishmonger truck rumbles behind the beach huts. The neon lights begin to hum as light spills out from the arcade. And as the sky gets lighter and the gulls get louder, the time comes for me too to take my place.

Ava exits. Josh replaces her, sprinting.

JOSH   You heard of the Domino Effect? It's a bit mad you know. In the war, Hitler had this plan – I can't remember the name – but it was basically where Aryan soldiers knocked up women in places like Scandinavia to make the next generation bare Aryan. So in 1945, this little baby girl is born to a Nazi soldier and a Norwegian woman. That little girl goes on to be one of the women in ABBA. So the next time your night out is ruined by some hen do screeching Dancing Queen, you can thank Hitler for that. I was up watching videos about it last night. Then I watched another, and another, and another. Anyway it gets to 3 am and I've fucked it, and now, I'm going to miss the bus. It's at the stop, and I think... David! (*Aside*) Friend from school. – David! Hold it! – He sees me.

David sees Josh running. He flips him off, then boards the bus.

JOSH   David, no! You fucking... Dickhead!

Josh catches his breath, hands on his knees.

JOSH   Piss take. Fucked now 'cause if you miss that eight-oh-seven bus out of town, you end up on the eight-twenty-two. And that's peak 'cause –

Josh is on the bus, packed in.

JOSH   It's just swamped with school uniforms. Just shrieking and cackling, on their way to this dusty old trailer park the council has the guts to call a school. The rest of us, like me, on our way to our own little ball and chain. The Chum Buddy Feed Factory – manufacturers of the finest dog food money can buy, according to... I don't know, dogs, I guess. It's this fat black fortress a few miles out of town, but employing almost a third of the workforce in it. Down the bus I spot Adi.

Adi appears on the bus. They nod to each other.

JOSH   My sister's boyfriend. Works at Chum Buddy too – assistant regional manager. They met at the town fete last year: Ava was running the Splat-A-Rat, Adi was splatting rats. A tale as old as time.

Josh joins Adi down the bus.

JOSH   Morning.

ADI   (*Sarcastically*) You're looking spritely – get a lucky scratch card or something?

JOSH   I can dream. You coming round tonight?

ADI   Of course. Fish and Chip Friday, wouldn't miss it for the world.

JOSH   Yeah, nice one. You reckon our fans are still waiting for us?

ADI   Yeah, definitely. Sheila in accounts sent through a video of them when she arrived this morning doing some dance around a soft toy. Not sure what it's supposed to mean.

JOSH   (*Aside*) Past few weeks the factory gates have been flanked by a couple dozen protestors shouting us all down as we walk into work. They got all these carboard signs their kids probably made for them in arts and crafts. 'Sink or Swim!' 'Prepare for Extinction!' 'Stop being fossil fools!' Cringe, mate. As if any of that shite's to do with me. (*To Adi*) Can't you just get security to remove them?

ADI   Well technically no because they're outside the gates so it's public land. And even if we could, they then call it a 'clash' and get the press coverage they want, more of the basement dwellers show up, and suddenly we're front-page news. Best to just let them get on with it. In other news, you hear about the Tandoori?

JOSH   What, they finally lower their prices?

ADI   No, not quite. Some prick spray painted some colourful slurs over the shutters.

JOSH   Oh, shit. You okay?

ADI   (*Laughs*) Yeah, I don't own the place, but thanks for checking in.

JOSH   Mr Joshi okay?

ADI   I've got no idea, Josh. You think the two village Asian get together before work and have a catch up over samosas or something?

JOSH   Nah, didn't mean it like that –

ADI   I'm messing with you. But no I've got no idea, just heard about it on my way in. Some scumbag. You got any idea who might have done it?

JOSH   In answer to the question you're wanting to ask, I haven't spoken to David or Seaweed in a couple weeks, so no.

ADI   Fair enough.

The bus pulls up, and they step off.

ADI   Anyway, you be a good boy. I'll see you later on.

JOSH   You take liberties, mate.

They peel off stage. Ava replaces them, at the end of her shift.

AVA   The last happy – ish – customer of the day finally vacates the café, and I flip the sign from 'Come in, the coffee's brewing!'

to 'Catch us in the morning!' Thursdays and Fridays are my long shifts, opening to close. Dawn, she's the owner, she shares the childcare for her grandson, so I help out here where I can. She's glamorous, Dawn, even when she's working. White hair pulled up by a polka-dot ribbon, her eyes shadowed pink, her lips bright red.

DAWN   I-do-not-bloody-be-*lieve*-it. Have you heard, Ava? They're only talking about building that bloody great nuclear power place down past Dinklage Point.

AVA   (*Aside*) Head of Swell's NWA, like a bouncer outside a nursing home, this is her domain.

DAWN   Chernobyl-on-sea, that's what they'll call us! I don't bloody well think so. You really must stay so vigilant these days. Blink once, and before you know it, the places you love are completely ruined.

AVA   You hear about the graffiti?

DAWN   Oh, don't - so uncouth! I was chatting to Caroline who sits on the Association with me, and she says that her boy – you know big Richard with the lisp? Well he heard at the pet shop today that Belinda - she's that one who's chihuahua got taken by the seagull– she was walking home from The Anchor last night and saw some hoodie running out from Shingle Street. She reckons it was them.

AVA   Is there not CCTV or anything?

DAWN   What are we, the Tower of London? Not here, love, none of it's actually connected to anything. Who's got time to pay for all that nonsense? Luckily it was just on the shutters. Mr Joshi was able to just roll them up before the visitors started arriving. Here, you give me that, love. I'll finish this off. Send my love to the boys.

Dawn peels off, as Ava leaves work.

AVA   Out on the street, the temperature drops as the breeze flits in from the sea. Down the high street I head to Art's. It's 6pm, and I'm starving. Enter the fishy, Arthur stands behind the counter, dirty white shirt and skin like worn leather.

ART   You alright doll, what'll it be? The usual?

AVA   Please, Art.

ART   Right on, doll, vamos.

AVA   Newspaper-wrapped bounty under my arm, I'm back out on the high street and heading home. I pass Mrs Marlowe, out for her evening stroll with her carer. She's barking mad, known as the Queen of Swell, but she's always liked me for some reason. She must be one of the richest people in the town, rumour has it her late husband used to own half the beach front, but you'd never know it looking at her in her moth-bitten brown cardigan.
And before I know it, on the other side of town, where Hill Road meets London Street... home. Top floor flat, the space me and Josh call ours.

We are taken inside. Josh and Adi are watching TV. They sit, looking somewhat dead, waiting for Ava's return. The sound of keys turning in the door.

ADI   Shit, she's back.

The boys jump out of their seats and rush to get the table ready.

AVA   (*Off*) Is the table all ready?

ADI   Yeah, been ready for ages!

Ava comes in just as they jump into their seats.

AVA   Bon appetit.

Time passes. They have finished their food. They sit at the table, letting it digest, with the TV still on in the background, the news playing quietly but audibly.

JOSH   - So they have this bucket of fake blood, and they're dipping their teddy bear in it, like, kinda violently. Then they passed the teddy bear on and the next person does the same, like that in a circle. Then when they're all done just violating this bear, they all start crying and weeping and shit. Start giving it a funeral.

AVA   Right.

JOSH   Something to do with the willful ignorance of the higher powers. Whatever the fuck that means.

AVA   I mean I get it, but is there not a bigger enemy than dog food?

JOSH   They got too much time on their hands. Should get a job.

AVA   Josh being a good boy at work?

JOSH   Oi, relax.

ADI   Yeah, he's secretly a little grafter. Your cool boy energy's not fooling us, mate.

JOSH   You don't even see me at work, what you on about?

ADI   I've got eyes everywhere mate, like Argus.

JOSH   Who?

ADI   Don't worry.

AVA   Think the best thing is to just ignore them, Josh. They'll be there till they got bored and find something else to protest about, some other factory. Just stay clear of them, no point doing something stupid.

JOSH   Who said I was gonna do something stupid?

AVA   No, I'm not saying you're going to do something stupid, I'm just saying. You know how you can be sometimes. A bit provocative.

JOSH   I'm not provocative.

AVA   You can be a little.

JOSH   No I'm not, I just don't have patience for people fucking me around.

AVA   Alright, intolerant then.

JOSH   What are you –

Something on TV has caught Adi's attention.

ADI   Wait, shh, turn that up.

The TV volume becomes clear.

AVA   Bloody hell, it's Swell!

JOSH   This about the graffiti?

NEWS   "...Swell is a well-known but small coastal retreat, welcoming
            almost two-hundred thousand visitors a year. But this whole
            town, every house, shop, street and sewer, is set to be
            demolished in the next fifty years, and returned to the sea..."

AVA   Wait, what?

NEWS   "This comes after a review by a local council taskforce into the
            sustainability of coastal communities in the wake of global
            sea levels rising. The council argue that certain towns like
            Swell, here on the east coast, are indefensible, with parts of
            the town lower than the sea level itself. A spokesperson from
            the council has said that 'this decommissioning of Swell is a
            devastating blow to the residents and tourists that come
            each year, but a forward-looking approach that's needed if we
            are to combat climate change.'"

JOSH   What the fuck's that mean?

AVA   What are they talking about decommissioning? What does that
            even mean?

ADI   That can't be right. We'd have heard.

AVA   It's on BBC, Adi. That sounds pretty damning.

ADI   But... We would've been told. Surely we would have been told?

The boys disappear and Ava is alone. The next day.

AVA   It felt like a sick joke. Like we'd wake up in the morning and
            be told it was all a big misunderstanding. Adi fell asleep as
            soon as his head hit the pillow, convinced it will all be clarified
            soon, but... I don't know.
            The next day I'm sat in the corner of the kitchen, picking at a
            house sandwich Dawn's whipped up for me. She's like a

flustered mother hen this morning, stuttering and puffing about the kitchen. (*To Dawn*) You okay, Dawn?

DAWN   Of course not, dear. How can any of us be? Shame on them for dropping something like that on us, on the BB-bloody-C of all places.

AVA   Adi thinks it's been blown out of proportion. Just something over nothing you know? He's probably right.

DAWN   Oh don't you worry. We had an emergency meeting this morning, seven o'clock they were   all in my garden. They're not going to get away with it, I'll tell you that for free. We've got plans. Blocks and vetoes. They're poking a hornet's nest thinking we're bumblebees, you'll see.

We see Josh leaving work, a few days later.

JOSH   Swell has this front of being a theme park for tourists to poke about, rather than being a real, breathing town, where people live, love, age, die and grieve. It's not just a weekend away or a headline in a travel column. Swell's my home, you know what I mean? When the news broke, a long few days ago now, that front began to crack. For the first time, people realised that maybe we are more important than our beach huts and town of the year awards. Maybe we should spend some actual energy worrying about this, rather than scrubbing off graffiti, just in case, God forbid, Swell is seen as a real place, with real actual people and actual problems. That wouldn't fit on a postcard though, I guess. Ava would tell me I'm being pessimistic. I'm not. I know this town as well as her, I just find myself in a different part of it.

ADI   (*Off*) Josh!

Adi enters.

JOSH   You alright?

ADI   We need to talk, but I need your discretion.

JOSH   What do you mean?

ADI We've just had a snap meeting with management. Like, management management. Look I don't know how to say this sensitively so I'm just gonna say it. They're moving the factory.

JOSH They're what?

ADI They've been in talks with the council, more than any of us have fucking got. When Swell goes –

JOSH So it is real?

ADI It's starting to sound that way. When Swell goes, the factory will be on the front line and the powers at be have written it off. They said it's not economically sustainable, or safe, they want to move it sooner rather than later.

JOSH Just like that?

ADI They were already under pressure to modernise, the factory's old, it's on dirty fuel. They were planning on investing here, but all this has been the final straw. There's no point.

JOSH What are you talking about? Where are they moving it?

ADI Somewhere low risk, cheap. I don't know yet.

JOSH Well what about all of us? They have a duty of care to –

ADI I don't know they're still working it out but... Look I just thought you should know. Give you a heads up.

JOSH They can't do that. The town needs this as much as any fucking café or shitty museum –

ADI You're right. But the town is dead, and they want to get away before the corpse starts to rot.

The scene changes. St Augustine's Church Hall.

JOSH After nine days of hearing fuck all from anyone official, the council decide they should probably let us know what's happening.

AVA The church hall at St Augustine's – normally only ever used for Zumba and kid's parties – is filled to the brim, the whole town packed inside like sardines. Everyone's here. Dawn sits with her grandson a few rows ahead –

DAWN (*To her grandson*) These cowboys are trying to take our town away, but they don't know they've got to deal with your granny first.

AVA On the other side of the hall Arthur leans against a beam –

ART Are we starting or what?

AVA Mrs Marlowe sits with her carer at the front, no doubt here two hours early –

MRS M The world's gone soft...

AVA And others too. Peggy with the fashion store on the high street, arms chained in silver bangles.

JOSH Mr Joshi sits near the back, quiet giant surrounded by stress.

AVA Phil from the butchers and Alan from the fishmongers.

JOSH Even David and Seaweed. I make eye contact, so now I've gotta go say hi. Now Seaweed obviously isn't his real name. He's never been a looker: pig nosed, greasy hair, and acne that covers him like acid rain. Someone once said that he was like seaweed, because not even the tide would take him out. It stuck, and he's owned it ever since. David's not even David's real name either, thinking about it. He's got real little man syndrome, used to pick on anyone bigger than him at school, start fights and that. So people started calling him David, as in Goliath. And they call me –

DAVID Y'all right, Mambo?

JOSH (*Aside*) I used to live at number five. (*To the boys*) How we doing?

DAVID Not bad, mate.

SEAW. Yeah, not bad, not bad.

JOSH Didn't expect to see you here.

DAVID Fuck all else to do, 'int there?

SEAW. Yeah, fuck all else to do.

DAVID Plus, might even get a bit beefy.

JOSH Doubt it, just some gimp the council's sent.

DAVID Ain't see you in ages, Mambo. Where you been hiding?

SEAW. Yeah, where you been hiding?!

JOSH   Not hiding, just been busy.

DAVID   What, chilling with your sister and her boyfriend? She still with that prick?

JOSH   He's not a prick.

DAVID   He is. Something about him.

SEAW.   Yeah, where you been mate? Come for a drink.

JOSH   I'll let you know.

The councilman arrives and takes to the lectern at the front of the hall. A weedy, pathetic man.

CMAN.   Th- th- thank you all for c- coming tonight. I understand the past week has been rather confusing, and of course, the, uh, the unfortunate broadcast –

ART   Get to the point! Vamos!

CMAN.   I certainly w- will, uh, yes. As you, unfortunately heard on the news the other night, S- Swell has been marked by the council and, uh, the, uh, government, as an irredeemable area due to the impact of f- flooding, owing to, of course, sea levels, which have been –

DAWN   This is our home!

AVA   What's happening to the town?

CMAN.   R- right of course. Of course. All excellent questions, and I- I- Let me settle those concerns for you. The current plan is that, owing to current predictions of 50 cm sea level rise, Swell will suffer, uh, ca- catastrophic flooding that will not be viable, uh, economically speaking, to defend. So the plan is to restore the area to a, uh, tidal salt marsh to protect the, the, the coastline and b- buffer the impacts –

AVA   So we're sacrificial lambs?

CMAN.   No, no, I can- I should have s- said, there will be the, uh, the opportunity for questions at the end, I do assure you. No, sacrificial lambs is, uh, rather dramatic. We are aiming to decommission the town, and by that we mean, uh, to abandon, deconstruct and de- depopulate between 2041 and 2051, depending, of course, on any f- future sea rise.

DAWN   And what's happening to our homes?

ART   And our businesses?

JOSH   What are you doing about our jobs?

The stage becomes bare. Ava sits alone, after the meeting, trying to gather her thoughts.

AVA   I was 18 when dad passed away. I came home from college one evening to find I couldn't open the front door, something was holding it. I thought Josh was mucking around but it just went on too long and it was too early for him to be home from school, anyway. I climbed over the garden fence and through the back. I found my dad by the front door, still warm, barely breathing. I called him an ambulance but by the time they arrived, he had   slipped from us. Just like that. One morning he's there, reading the same book he'd been reading forever in the corner of the conservatory. The next minute, he's just gone. Heart attack. No warning.

When I was ten, Josh would've been eight, Dad bought us this remote-control airplane for Christmas. He used to buy us expensive presents back then, I think he was trying to make up for mum leaving us. Silly. We went down to the beach and started flying it, and Josh decided he was going to be a pilot (*she laughs.*) Dad must not have charged it as much as he thought he did because at one point we're flying it and it just stops. The propellers on it go dead and it starts gliding out to sea. Well Dad, he goes sprinting into the ocean, absolutely freezing December ocean, fully clothed in his big coat, and just starts fighting his way through the tide to catch it. And he did. For us, he managed. He came back and we sat on the pebbles and just hugged him so tight whilst he caught his breath.

Every part of this town, my Dad sits in its corners, on its curbs and its cafes and pubs. Every sunrise stroll I say good morning to him, tell him how I'm doing. You can't have Swell without my Dad... and you can't have my Dad without Swell.

They talk about decommissioning the town. How can you decommission a town? You decommission a factory, or a

machine. Not peoples' lives. Not peoples' homes and
memories. That's not right.

Adi enters, cautiously.

ADI   Can we have a chat?

Ava composes herself, taken off guard.

AVA   Yeah, of course.

ADI   You okay?

AVA   Yeah, all good. What's up?

ADI   I need you to hear me out before you respond, okay? I had a
            meeting with my manager today. The factory isn't going to
            move for another 18 months, but they're already planning for
            it. The next 18 months will be a gradual wind down until
            operations cease. In the meantime though, I've been offered a
            promotion.

AVA   Adi, that's incredible! Congratulations!

ADI   Thank you. But... It's not here.

AVA   Oh. Where is it?

ADI   Scotland.

AVA   Oh. That's very much not here.

ADI   And it's conditional. They want me ready for the next quarter.

Pause.

AVA   So what are you saying then?

ADI   Just hear me out. I've been thinking about it, and this whole
            thing's going to have huge implications, Ava. I think it would
            be foolish to not take them up on it, so I've said I'll take it.

AVA   So you're just going up and off to Scotland, like that? I thought
            you were angry about what they're doing here?

ADI   It's not 'just like that' Ava, I've thought hard about it. And I am
            angry –

AVA	Well you're not. First chance you're given you're fucking off, getting out whilst you can. Christ, Adi, it's not even been two weeks –
ADI	That we've known about it but this has been in motion for months. We were just the last to hear about it.
AVA	You're still upheaving your whole life in the space of a fortnight!
ADI	Ava, please think it through. There isn't another option. I stay here, in 18 months I'm made redundant and the offer of a good job, fuck, the offer of *any* job here is gone. What do you expect me to do, sell buckets and spades on the beach?
AVA	And what about me?
ADI	I was hoping you might think about coming with me.
AVA	To Scotland? With the bagpipes and biannual independence vote? No, Adi, I'm not moving to Scotland. I'm not flipping my life upside down just because you've shat the bed.
ADI	Ava, I'm not –
AVA	You could stay here at fight for this community with me. That's your other option, Adi. We could stop this.
ADI	Please, Ava, you're living in a bubble. I cannot stay here, nobody can.
AVA	I should've seen this coming. This has never been your home, has it? Just a place you lived.
ADI	Fucks sake, Ava, don't be so unfair. This place isn't my home like yours, no, how can it be? You talk about saving this community – half this community don't look at me the same way they look at you and Josh. Some of them are actively uncomfortable. What am I saving?
AVA	What? Is this because of the graffiti? Some racist arsehole –
ADI	Ava, it's not about the fucking graffiti. It's about this place. This is bigger than me and you do you not get that? I want us to figure something out. I don't want to lose you –
AVA	If you meant that, you'd have spoken to me first.
ADI	I am speaking to you.

AVA	No, you're telling me. If I asked you to stay, would you?
ADI	I don't think you would.
AVA	You're right. I wouldn't. And nor would you.

Silence. They both know what it means.

AVA	I'd like you to leave, Adi.
ADI	Ava, please can we just –
AVA	Leave! Get the fuck out of my flat!

The scene changes. Ava is left alone on stage. Time has passed.

| JOSH | (*Off*) Ava, did you move my toothbrush? |
| AVA | It's on charge, Josh. |

Josh enters, sees Ava melancholy.

JOSH	You alright?
AVA	Just thinking about him, I'm fine.
JOSH	Oh.
AVA	Have you heard from him at all?
JOSH	Yeah.

Ava nods.

| AVA | Good of him to message you and not me. |
| JOSH | You made it pretty clear you didn't want anything to do with him. |

Ava shrugs. A pause.

| AVA | And what about you? |

JOSH   What about me?

AVA   You know. What are you going to do? You're in the same boat.

Josh sighs.

JOSH   I'm not leaving you, Ava. Where would I go? I wouldn't have a clue. I'm staying. This is my home too, and... well I don't really have anyone else, do I?. I'm going to have to figure it out in 18 months, aren't I? But I won't be angry at Adi like you want me to be. He didn't have a choice, and it's wrong of you to pretend he did. And I think there'll come a time where we wish we had gone with him too.

Act Two

Three years later.

AVA   Like a calendar in a hurricane, the dates start flying.

JOSH   Days into weeks, weeks into months, and somehow months into years.

AVA   That foggy fortnight like a bad taste, desperately trying to reverse it and prevent it, but nothing working.

JOSH   Peggy was the first to go, down on the high street. Within a few weeks of the announcement she'd packed up her shop and retreated. She's got these boutiques up and down the coast – what's the point in investing in a dying economy?

AVA   After that the whole town was a game of retail musical chairs. The music stops and the next business is boarded up.

JOSH   Occasionally redeveloped, but it's like they leave a curse. Once the original goes, none are staying for long.

AVA	After that, everyone's paranoid. Gossips and sharp words shared over a shandy in the pub, everybody drawing up their own naughty and nice lists of who cares enough to stay, and who's wise enough to leave. A quasi-nationalistic pride for a town put on death row.
ART	What'll it be, doll, the usual?
AVA	Thanks, Arthur. You hear about Peggy?
ART	Ah, fuck Peggy. Her eyes never did rest in this town. I won't be going nowhere, don't you worry. Long as there's fish to fry, you'll find me behind this counter.
AVA	Other anxieties attack elsewhere.
DAWN	I could bloody kill those councilmen, you know.
AVA	What's happened?
DAWN	After fifteen bloody months of them stringing us a long, they turn around and say we have no jurisdiction for government decisions. Still, that ridiculous plan to build a power plant down at Dinklage point has been abandoned. Small victories, I'll take them!
AVA	Then the factory shut.
JOSH	Over 600 of us, hands wiped clean. Every job in town sucked up, but nowhere enough for us all. And I was one of the lucky ones, sort of.
AVA	Why's that, Josh?
JOSH	Well, I end up working for Seaweed at the arcade, don't I? I get on with the lad but... It's like working for a kid who treats his whole life like it's Xbox Live. He gave it a whole lot of –
SEAW.	Don't worry, Mambo. I may be your boss but doesn't mean we can't still be friends outside. I don't want things to be awkward.
JOSH	- And sometimes he'd ask –
SEAW.	Do you mind oiling up the claw machine a bit? It's got too tight, Too many kids with prizes.
JOSH	- And more and more it was –

SEAW. Before you ask me, I know I owe you for last month, it'll be with you in a few days, max.

JOSH It's what he said last month too. And so eventually, I said, (*to Seaweed*) Alright, fuck off, Seaweed! Pay what you owe me and shove your tokens up your arse, I don't need this shit anymore.

SEAW. (*Pause*) Where's that come from?

JOSH Around that time I get a call from Adi. He's regional manager now, earning good money. Wants me to join his team, says I'd be a great fit. I declined it, and I kept the call to myself. Don't get me wrong, I was buzzing. Nobody's ever believed in me like that but... My dad used to say to me, a house divided can't stand a storm. Can't leave Ava, not right now, so I stayed put.

AVA The town begins to bruise. In the first week property drops 40%, like a body bag in the sea. No warning, no precedent. Then the other three horsemen trot into the picture. No mortgages, no insurance, no investment. Pushed into a death spiral that nobody can navigate, that nobody has ever *had* to navigate before.

JOSH A second visit from the council does fuck all to help anyone.

CMAN. We thought it, uh, important, to call this, uh, this meeting, to clarify a few points. On the issue of, uh, of compensation and, and, and financial assistance... Well there's really nothing that can be done, unfortunately –

AVA You've decommissioned our home and you're doing nothing to help us?

CMAN. Well, um, that's, uh... The problem is, that, uh, rising sea levels are really nobody's... you know, nobody's fault, so there does come an issue in, in, in sourcing compensation –

ART Source it from our fucking taxes, vamos!

CMAN. I really would ask, that we all, j- j- just keep calm, and listen to the plans we have laid out.

AVA You haven't got any!

JOSH Shit stops getting fixed. A house needs repainting. Why bother? A kitchen needs replacing. This one'll do. A drunk driver crashes into a resident's fence? Always wanted to see the road anyway.

AVA Tourists start dwindling in numbers, put off by the receding aestheticism of the town. Not a huge amount, but we're only small, and we feel it enough to panic people more.

JOSH Ava somehow pulls through and gets me a job at the little vanity museum in the town square. Not where I thought I'd be at 22, but... Well, beggars can't be choosers init. So now, here I am. The smiling face of Swell's history and culture, for anyone who pays six pounds and gives a shit.

AVA And before we know it we've wasted three years of our lives fighting off a decision that was never going to fight back, because it didn't need to. It was settled before we'd even heard of it. And so we drop out of limbo and try to restructure some semblance of normality. Me, still at the café, Josh at the museum. Between us barely making enough to cover rent.

Time moves as the dust settles.

AVA I'm in Remembrance Square, two bags of shopping for Mrs Marlowe. Her old carer left in the most recent exodus, and her new one is only part-time, so I volunteered to grab her shopping when I'm needed. As I head back to the west-end, I turn right down my usual cut-through, but as I turn I find three boys down the alley, hoods up, resting on bikes, a fag in each of their hands. A new fixture in our otherwise quiet, quiescent town. Their just children, really, it's pathetic. But I turn around and back down towards the High Street instead. Within ten minutes I'm at her front door. She's stood there, waiting.

MRS M Thanking you, poppet.

AVA Mrs M's house is like walking into an old rerun of Corrie. Frilly white curtains turned brown in the sun cover thin wood-chipped windows. A crimson-and-yellow carpet covers the entire living room like an interior designer vomited and left the mess. And yet as you scan the room, small whispers of her wealth emerge. On the walls are photos of her and her late husband. One stands out to me, taken in front of the beach huts, some sixty years ago. Through her clouded grey eyes, Mrs M senses me looking.

MRS M My Ralph.

AVA - She tells me. She gives me the story. Her father used to send her and her sisters to Swell when they were growing up –

MRS M Not like now, everyone goes abroad.

AVA - She met Ralph at a dance when she was 15. There used to be a dance hall –

MRS M Tesco's car park, now.

AVA - Ralph was with his friend, Don, at this dance, and everyone was in love with Don. But Mrs M was drawn to Ralph from the moment she first saw him, because –

MRS M He was quiet. Ugly.

AVA When she turned 17, she moved down to Swell to be with him. They got married in St Augustine's, and she's lived in the same house ever since.

MRS M Ralph's still here, no doubts.

AVA That's when she picks up this pristine little box off the side cabinet and opens it for me.

MRS M (*Struggling to open it*) Bastard.

Music softly plays from the box.

AVA It's beautiful, a figure of a ballerina pirouetting on a yellow cushioned stage. Mrs M tells me she's –

MRS M Got loads of them.

AVA Ralph used to buy them for her, and she's never thrown a single one. All she has to do to feel Ralph with her is open a box, and it takes her back to a real time with him. (*To Mrs M*) You have such beautiful memories here, Mrs Marlowe.

MRS M Well, I'm not leaving.

AVA   (*Softly*) We might not have much of a choice one day.

MRS M My Ralph was here in '53. Floods. Escaped onto his roof with his baby sister to survive. Swell got through that, that were no tea party. Suddenly we can't defend against floods? Pfft. World's gone soft.

Mrs Marlowe peels off stage.

AVA   When I'm finally able to peel myself away, I check my watch to find I'm running late. Shit. I pace it down London Street and take a left at the beachfront. As I reach the beach huts, passing graffiti that dried weeks ago, I see Josh waiting up ahead.

Josh appears, carrying two coffee cups.

JOSH   Hey.

AVA   Hey, I'm so sorry I'm late. I was helping Mrs M, and she wouldn't –

JOSH   It's cool. I brought hot chocolate.

He hands her a cup. Ava breathes out her tension, then gives Josh a hug.

AVA   Thank you.

JOSH   How was she?

AVA   Mrs M? She was Mrs M. Think she thinks its millennials fault the town is being condemned. We're too sheltered, apparently. How you doing?

JOSH   Not bad, you?

AVA   I'm doing just fine.

They take a seat and sit close together, watching the ocean as it laps against the shore.

JOSH	I never come down here, you know. Forget how nice it is.
AVA	It's God's garden, I'm telling you. People travel miles to be in places like this. It's on our back door.
JOSH	Makes me feel very small.
AVA	With everything going on, this is the only part of town that feels exactly the same as it's always been.

A seagull shrieks above them, and they watch it fly.

JOSH	You know, I had a thought. Don't you think its dumb that the tourists hate seagulls?
AVA	What do you mean?
JOSH	Well, tourists don't like the gulls because they swoop down and act like what's yours is theirs. To me, a seagull is just a tourist with wings.

Ava laughs. Josh laughs also.

AVA	They're not bad, Josh.
JOSH	Nah, I know. You notice them when they're gone.
AVA	How's work?
JOSH	Excruciatingly shit. I'm just sat on a stall for like, eight hours a day, doing nothing. Occasionally someone will have a question for me, but Andy never actually gave me any training, so I just end up making shit up. Funnest part of my day, that.
AVA	Well, if you're looking for something to keep you entertained, you could always join me on a Tuesday evening. Litter picking then tea and cakes after.
JOSH	Said I was bored, not desperate. Christ, can't believe you actually just suggested that to me. I'd rather peel off my fingernails.

Ava laughs.

AVA   You sure you're holding up okay?

JOSH   (*Shrugs*) Just feel angry so much of the time. Angry at what they've done to this place. Angry at the community for not fighting back hard enough. Angry at myself for where I am.

AVA   Hey, stop that. We've been dealt a shit hand, Josh, and you've handled everything like a champ. Dad would be proud of you.

JOSH   Don't know about that. I'm not the golden child am I, doing charity work every day of the week.

AVA   It's not every day, Josh. It just keeps me busy, nothing more to it.

JOSH   Nah for real, he'd be mad proud of you. I've been thinking about him a lot this week. I was thinking about that time you had your orchestra recital when you were like, eleven, do you remember?

AVA   (*Laughing*) How could I forget?

JOSH   Spent hours trying to herd us into the car and we just wouldn't cooperate. Finally gets us there with seconds to spare, and realises you've left your violin at home.

They enjoy the memory.

AVA   Bless him, that was him though, wasn't it? Through and through. He was just trying so hard for us, and we must have been like juggling two hot potatoes.

JOSH   I'm not glad he's gone; I don't mean that. But... it's a relief, you know? That he's not here to see what's happening to us now. To see how what's going on.

AVA   He'd be devastated. No doubt he'd be telling people down The Anchor how he'd be growing gills before they forced him out his home.

A pause.

JOSH   I miss him.

AVA   So do I.

Josh raises his cup in a toast.

JOSH   Happy birthday, Dad.

AVA   Happy birthday.

Time moves on.

JOSH   The weeks move by slower than before. Every day it feels like
            this town gets smaller. It always happens at the end of season,
            but this is something different. Just a vicious cycle.
            I'm sat on my stall, in an empty museum on a wet October
            afternoon, wondering how the fuck I got here. Leaving
            Seaweed's circus felt like the right move at the time, but
            finding work around here now's like finding lemonade in your
            piss. Still, Ava pulled through. She does this green conscience
            thing with Andy, the manager here, and she was able to wing
            me this gig. She saved the day. As she always does.
            I remember when I was seven mum ran off with this guy, just,
            like, disappeared on us one night. My sister was hugging me
            one night because I just wouldn't stop crying, and she said,
            "I'll never forgive her for leaving you." Leaving <u>me.</u> It wasn't
            about her, and it never has been. She left college just to see me
            out of school. And she'd do that for anyone. Even I know that's
            rare.
            The door creaks open and I watch a family come in. Four of
            them, speaking some foreign language I don't know. They're
            all overweight, chicken wings spilling over tight vests, except
            for the dad, who's built like Slenderman in a Patagonia jacket.
            Guy looks like he has wet dreams over military history.
            The daughter immediately falls onto the bench, feet swung
            over the side like it's a fucking therapist's office, and gets
            texting. Fantastic use of £6. The mum goes from plaque to
            plaque, not really taking anything in, looking at the photos but
            not much else. The dad though, oh boy. You can tell who's
            choice it was to be here. Every little small print, every sub-
            headline and curator information he's taking in like the man's
            just discovered he can smell. I'm so engrossed in thinking up

bullshit facts to give them that I barely notice his podgy little son sprinting past me into the aquarium. I say aquarium, it's really a dozen tanks filled with some pretty dead local fish. And the octopus. Yeah, he's pretty sick to be fair. The kid starts tapping on the tanks, chasing some bream with his greasy little fingers.

(*To the kid*) Oi! You can't tap the tanks. (*Speaking slower and gesturing*) You cannot touch the tanks.

He shrugs and moves on. The dad's still sniffing the words, enjoying the Dunkirk plaque. It's funny, my own dad brought me here once when I was kid, and I remember thinking about what things I'd live through here that would end up on these walls. Now, nothing. It's all just... stopped. The mum's frowning at pictures from the '53 floods, looking unimpressed by our death toll. I guess that's what they mean when they talk about catastrophic flooding, but I don't know. We haven't had a flood here since the 90s, and it should be getting worse. But the scientists reckon they've got it all -

My train of thought is derailed by the kid in the aquarium, poking the glass like it's a game of fucking Candy Crush.

(*To the kid*) Hey! No. No tapping! You cannot tap, it scares the fish.

Prick. The parents are either none the wiser or confidently do not give a shit that their son is running around like a fucking sports day. The dad's still enjoying our tragedies, the mum now with the daughter on her phone. Can they not hear me telling their kid to behave?

And as I'm staring at them wondering what's good, Augustus Gloop comes back into my peripheral vision. He's jabbing once again, this time at the octopus, who's darted behind his rock to hide from this giant fucking baby. And I don't know what it is about this kid in this moment, and this one and only family of the day, but as I look at him I see very thoughtless visitor in that fat fucking index finger, every tap like a headache, and before I even know what I'm doing I'm over there. I grab his wrist, pull it back, and yell -

STOP POKING THE TANKS YOU LITTLE FUCKING DICKHEAD!

A pause. A high pitching ringing. It settles.

JOSH   The kid starts crying. I turn around to see his parents at the door, shell-shocked. His sister filming it. On the other side of the room, Andy, out of his office.

ANDY   Josh, can I speak to you in my office, right now.

JOSH   Fuck.

Josh goes off stage into Andy's office, head sunken. We see Ava at work.

AVA   Outside it's black. A starless sky, softly spitting and beating against the front windows. My reflection only fractured by the flickering floodlights out on the street. Alone, save for the company of Otis Redding, playing quietly from the speakers. With no customers, I use this time for myself.

Taking stock, the past few years feel little more than a fever dream. Petitions and protests and pages of precious opinions published, but all for nothing. The town will sink, and with it we either drown or learn to swim. So we do. Those of us who are still too stubborn to sacrifice our homes do what we can to keep the community afloat.

But with the tide calming it becomes clearer to see our position in it all – <u>my</u> position in it all. 24 years old and still the Corner Café girl, a job I enjoy but not one I wanted to fill forever. So with these quiet nights on the high street, I look back into the possibility of returning to college. A nursing degree dumped because of dad's passing, now at a point in my life where I feel like I could return. I could do it. Every month I've been putting money aside. A small investment for a big future. It might mean leaving Swell and Dad but... I'd be doing something bigger. And I know that's what he'd want, so it wouldn't be leaving him behind. Not really. Nobody here needs me anymore.

The sound of a bell dinging. Two men, dressed in black with masks on, enter the café. One carries a knife in his pocket, the other a metal baseball bat. Ava stands, like a rabbit in headlights.

AVA   Can I help you?

MAN 1   You still open?

AVA   (*Quietly*) Yes.

MAN 1   That's good news. (*To Man 2*) You want anything to eat?

MAN 2   Nah, I've just eaten.

MAN 1   That's a shame. (*To Ava*) He's just eaten.

MAN 2   Nice caff you've got here. Good spot. Must get a lot of feet in and out.

MAN 1   I think we'll skip the pleasantries and get to the bit where you show us to your safe.

AVA   Excuse me?

MAN 2   Did he stutter?

Man 2 pulls the knife out and takes a suggestive step forwards.

MAN 2   Where's your fucking safe?

MAN 1   Relax. (*To Ava*) This doesn't have to be difficult.

AVA   Under the sink.

MAN 1   Code?

AVA   03-05.

MAN 1   Thank you, sweetheart.

The two men disappear off stage.

AVA   Her grandson's birthday. I think of Dawn as they strip her kitchen. Dawn, who has always looked after me. Dawn, who leaves me by myself on Thursdays and Fridays. The long shift. The landline sits resting by the register.

A pause. Then Ava rushes forward. She grabs the phone, and starts dialing 999.

MAN 2   (*From nowhere*) You stupid bitch!

He hits her, and throws her to the ground. He goes to kick her, but Man

1 intervenes.

MAN 1   Enough lets fucking go! (*Man 2 exits*). Fucks sake.

As they leave, Man 2 smashes windows in anger. They run off, and Ava is left alone, trembling, on the floor. The lights go down on her and we see Josh at home, pacing, frustrated. A door clicks open, Ava is home. Josh stands still, his head in his hands.

JOSH   Ava, I'm in here. I need to talk to you about something.

Ava appears at the door, her face wet with tears. She breaks down on seeing Josh.

JOSH   Ava, hey, what's happened!? What's wrong.

He embraces her. Ava tries to speak but cannot get her words out.

JOSH   Hey, calm down. It's all good. You're safe. Breathe.

Ava breaths in, deeply, and steadies her breathing.

AVA   These men came to the café and- and they had a knife and-

JOSH   Are you hurt?

AVA   They hit me but I'm okay –

JOSH   What?! Where did they kick you? Ava sit down, are you okay? You need to be checked over, there could be –

AVA   The police came. A medic looked over me. It's just bruising, nothing serious. I tried to reach the phone to get help, but they got to me first and –

JOSH   What? Why on earth would you risk that, Ava? Why put yourself in that position?

AVA   They took everything, Josh.

JOSH	They could've taken a lot more if they hadn't stopped at just a kick. What's the matter with you?
AVA	I wasn't thinking.
JOSH	What did you say to the police?
AVA	I told them everything I could remember, they're looking into it. There have been a couple other burglaries in the last few months, the garage and some houses up by the green. They think maybe it's the same people.
JOSH	They can't have gone far. Fucks sake, man. Fucking... scumbags. Fuck.

A pause as Josh processes it all.

AVA	Sorry, I was just in shock. I'm okay, really. What was it you needed to talk to me about?

Josh stops. He goes stiff, suddenly coming back to himself.

JOSH	Huh?
AVA	You wanted to talk to me about something. When I came in.
JOSH	Oh. I think that should probably wait.
AVA	No, go on, what's up?
JOSH	Seriously, it's not that deep.
AVA	So tell me.

Josh scrambles for the words to say.

JOSH	I, um... I- I lost my job.
AVA	What?
JOSH	I lost my job. I got fired.
AVA	Is this a joke? How did you get fired?
JOSH	I think... Well. I think I assaulted a child, is the official line.
AVA	Excuse me?

JOSH	I mean, it wasn't really an assault, just like a grab, but... I guess it doesn't make much difference on paper.
AVA	You assaulted a child?! Josh, what the fuck is wrong with you?
JOSH	I didn't mean to –
AVA	You can't accidentally commit assault.
JOSH	No, I'm not saying that. It all happened bare quick and I kept telling this kid to stop, but he just kept –
AVA	So you're on your arse again then? Unemployed?
JOSH	I mean –
AVA	It's not a particularly grey area, Josh, you are. Andy was doing us a favour –
JOSH	He was hardly Thomas fucking Bernardo, Ava, I was on minimum wage.
AVA	You were employed!
JOSH	(*Getting angry*) I'm 22 on minimum fucking wage!
AVA	So are most people! I'm 24 and I've been working in the same café for four years for you!
JOSH	For me? I didn't ask you to look after me –
AVA	But I did. And I've never stopped because you're still a child. You're 22 but still act like a boy, Josh.
JOSH	Excuse me, who the fuck do you think you are?
AVA	I'm your sister, Josh, but sometimes I feel like your fucking mum. If it wasn't for me, you'd be down The Anchor every night pissing away your future with David and Seaweed.
JOSH	Is that how you see me? Like some kind of bum?
AVA	I didn't say you were a bum –
JOSH	You think I started work because of you? You think I keep myself out of trouble because of you? Yes, you're my sister, but you're not my saviour. I stayed in this shit hole for you!
AVA	You didn't have a choice.
JOSH	Yes I did.
AVA	No you didn't -

JOSH   I did. Adi offered me a job. It was an opportunity to actually start something –

AVA   What are you talking about, when?

JOSH   - And instead I stayed here to look after *you*. I stayed here, working at a fucking arcade and a two-room museum, so that you wouldn't be alone.

All built up frustration and anger spills out from one to the other. Ava looks at Josh in shock.

JOSH   Do you not get it? This town is dead, Ava. It's dead. You're going to throw away your whole life and for what? And I've been stupid enough to be dragged down with you. This community is just fucking leeches, man. We could've got out when it first started, we could have gone when Adi left –

AVA   You think this is how I imagined my life? You're not the only one who's been let down.

JOSH   Why have you not already?

AVA   Life gets away from you. Yesterday I found Dad in the doorway and today we're here. I had to support you between the factory and the arcade, between the arcade and the museum, now I've got to support you again –

JOSH   I'm such a burden, am I?

AVA   Yes, Josh, when you're unemployed, you are! What do we do now?

JOSH   I'll find a job.

AVA   How? Where? I can't keep coming to your rescue every time you fuck up and lose your job.

JOSH   I don't need you to rescue me, I'm not a child. Worry about yourself for a fucking change.

The scene changes suddenly. The sound of sea gulls flying. Ava and Dawn sit outside the café together.

DAWN   Ava, I'm so sorry. I don't know what to say.

AVA   I'm so sorry I couldn't stop it.

DAWN   What on God's earth are you apologising for? I can't get over what scum would do this. Although we all know who, don't we? One of those bloody gypsies that have taken over the caravan park. It's disgusting to see what they've done to that place.

AVA   Travellers.

DAWN   Pardon?

AVA   We call them travellers these days.

DAWN   Oh toss what you're supposed to bloody say! I've owned that café thirty years, now look what they've done to it. What this town's become. I thought better of people. I believed in human decency at the minimum. Seems we're all out of that now.

AVA   I'm sure the police will find them, whoever it was.

DAWN   (*Scoffs*) Don't make me laugh. They're far too busy fining people on bloody scooters to give a toss about real crime. I blame myself. Me and the Association, we should have pushed harder when that lot took over that campsite. We knew they'd be nothing but trouble. Council told us they have rights too. Yeah well, look at my rights. Look at yours, last night.

AVA   We don't know it was them Dawn. There's no point speculating.

DAWN   Who else would it be? We didn't have problems like this before they moved in.

AVA   Maybe not this loud, but we did. We always did, Dawn.

A pause.

DAWN   I need to talk to you, sweetheart.

AVA   Right...

DAWN   I've seen everything on this corner. I've put my all into this place, Ava, everything I've got. But footfall's down, bad. And the bills aren't budging... I'm trying to help put my grandson through private school and my daughter's moving away and I –

AVA   What are you saying, Dawn?

DAWN   They've taken everything from me. What with the safe, and the repairs. The kitchen was already falling apart, but now this? I can't do it anymore. I can't afford it. And I can't be away from my grandson.

AVA   So what happens now?

DAWN   I'm selling. The council will take it off my hands, bastards won't give me near what I paid for it but... nobody else will buy the place. I don't have a choice. I'm done. This town. The bloody NWA. I can't do it anymore. I'm so sorry, Ava.

AVA   (*Nodding sadly*) I understand.

The stage becomes split. Josh and Ava fill the two halves, separately.

JOSH   From door to door, 'no' becomes the word of the day, everyday. Places that know me, places that knew my dad. Nobody can help. There isn't any work and even if there was, they've all the heard the story. They don't want me working for them, representing what little business they still have.

AVA   I find myself questioning whether it was something we did, or perhaps something we didn't do. Were there warning signs that we ignored, or some initiative we could have led to protect ourselves? I know the answer. The truth is we're passive victims of a faceless tragedy, but for me to accept that, I have to accept that I'm no more responsible for where I end up than a paper bag being beaten by the wind. And I'm not sure I'm ready to accept that yet.

JOSH   (*Imitating*) Joshua hit a child, did you hear? This poor little boy couldn't speak English, and Joshua just attacked him. Have you seen the video? It's ever so scary. My daughter heard from a class mate that her sister found it on the Twitter, #NotSoSwell. Just what we need, isn't it? Idiot boy.

AVA   Behind on rent, keeping afloat only by decimating what I had put away. Like that, any plans I may have had ripped from me just to keep our home. Both of us driftwood, just waiting to see where the stream dumps us.

The scene changes. It's late at night. Josh sits on the beach with David and Seaweed, whilst Seaweed sprays paint on the front of a beach hut. David drinks something rancid.

DAVID   Here mate, have some.

JOSH   Looks cheap.

DAVID   That's the point.

Josh takes a swig.

JOSH   That is fucking rank.

DAVID   Sorry, princess. Beggars can't be choosers. How's your sister?

JOSH   What?

DAVID   Heard about the job.

JOSH   Yeah, she's pretty shaken.

DAVID   (*Shakes his head*) Proper shame it went down that way.

SEAW.   And voila!

He turns to show them his graffiti.

JOSH   What's that?

SEAW.   It's my tag. Seaweed.

JOSH   It's three green lines.

SEAW.   Yeah, it's abstract.

JOSH   It's not abstract, it's shit.

SEAW.   Oi do one. What are you, the fucking graffiti police?

JOSH   Nah, I reckon that would just be the police. Did you have to do it on the hut?

DAVID   Why you so uptight, mate? Relax. It's a fucking beach hut, who gives a shit?

JOSH   (*Shrugs*) Don't know. Could at least do something artistic.

SEAW.   I'm not made of money, dickhead. Do you know how much this paint costs?

JOSH   Not a clue.

DAVID   Could always pay for it out of your cash bonuses, eh mate?

SEAW.   (*Laughs*) Yeah. Yeah, cash bonuses.

JOSH   What you talking about?

DAVID   Our Seaweed here's started sifting a bit of extra income from the machines at the end of the day.

JOSH   So you're stealing?

SEAW.   Nah. It ain't stealing. I'm top of the chain. You can't steal from top of the chain.

JOSH   Well you're not the owner.

SEAW.   Mate, that prick has 18 of those gaffs around the country. You think he misses the odd tenner out of Swell?

JOSH   Probably not.

SEAW.   It's a performance bonus, signed off by me. It ain't fucking stealing.

JOSH   Calm down, mate. What's your problem?

DAVID   What's *your* problem, Mambo? You're all stiff like a dead rabbit.

JOSH   I'm not.

DAVID   You are.

JOSH   I'm fucking not!

DAVID   You're like a kettle left to boil. If you don't take yourself off the heat, you're gonna blow mate. We all saw that at the museum.

JOSH   Yeah, fuck you.

DAVID   Seaweed's right though. That twat earns thousands across his different arcades, you know what I mean? He could be paying Seaweed better, especially given the shit creek we're all in down here, but he chooses not to. So Seaweed takes the odd bullseye out the fruity at the end of the day, who's he really hurting? Not even a dent for the man at the top, whilst for Seaweed... Well that's a meal out for the missus. If he had a missus, like.

JOSH   Whatever.

DAVID   We're all just trying to figure out if we're waving or drowning down here, mate. Been dealt a shit hand, no question. But everything after that's just a matter of choice. Do you choose to take it lying down, or do you choose to take back what control you can?

Josh grunts.

DAVID   Keep that bottle, I got another in my bag.

JOSH   How are you doing it?

DAVID   What do you mean?

JOSH   You don't have a job. How you getting by?

DAVID   You gotta find your own work sometimes. Like I said. All we have left is our choices.

A pause.

SEAW.   (*To Josh*) Here mate, have a go.

JOSH   You're good.

SEAW.   Oh go on, mate. Let loose a bit. Who's it hurting, really?

Josh considers this. He then stands up, takes the spray can, and starts to spray against the beach hut. As he does so the scene changes. Ava brings on a bag of shopping, and Mrs Marlowe waddles over.

AVA   Mrs M asks me how it is out there. She doesn't go out in winter, and her eyesight is getting worse by the day. Cataracts like a smoke screen. I tell her it's freezing, that the wind off the sea is slicing through the town like cheese wire.

MRS M When's the café back? Weeks now!

AVA Oh. Well, it's not, Mrs Marlowe.

MRS M Eh?

AVA After the theft and everything... We couldn't afford to keep it open. It's all boarded up now.

MRS M Gone?

AVA Yeah, gone, unfortunately. (*Aside*) She tells me she's sad about that, because she used to enjoy the Shephard's Pie we served, which is strange, because I've never seen Mrs M in the café, and we've never served Shephard's Pie.

MRS M What now?

AVA For me? Nothing, at the moment. Between jobs they call it.

MRS M You're a nurse.

AVA Well, no, not technically. I trained to be one for a couple of years, but I never finished the course.

MRS M My lady. She's going to leave.

AVA Leave?

MRS M Leave. Pooft. Another one bites the dust.

AVA When?

MRS M Week's end.

AVA Oh gosh, I'm sorry I had no idea. So what are you going to do?

MRS M They want to put me in a home. (*She laughs a dry, wheezy laugh.*) Bastards. Maybe we help each other.

AVA As in... What, I care for you?

MRS M (*Affirmatively*) Mm.

AVA Oh, it's very sweet of you to ask, but I'm not qualified. I never finished the course so –

MRS M Agh! Money for a certificate.

AVA But what about your medicines and –

MRS M I know my medicines. You read. Can you read?

AVA Yes.

MRS M Microwave?

AVA   Yeah, I know how to use a microwave.

MRS M Good. Week Monday?

AVA   Are you sure?

Mrs Marlowe gives an affirmative grunt and waddles off. Ava lets out a sigh of relief, then peels off stage.

JOSH   Knock knock. Hi I was wondering if – Not today son. Knock knock. Hi how you doing, my name's Josh – Bell rings. Hey Art how are you – I'm afraid nothing here, lad, vamos. Ring ring. Can we see a recent reference please? I don't think so. Knock knock, ring ring. Hi can I – what if I just – well if you have any vacancies – what about small things around the house – well here's my number. Knock knock. Hi I think you used to know my dad – I don't know you. Ring, ding, knock, knock. I'm just looking for – I understand – I'm a jack of all trades really – any small jobs you have – no worries have a good day. Knock knock, door shut, shutters down, ring ring, not today son. Fucking scraps! Stuck to my waist in quicksand but it's slow like the eight-twenty-two bus. No idea where I go from here, like a fucking Satnav with the batteries out. And Ava, of course, landing on her feet. As ever. The shining knight of the community somehow finding her way, but not me. Not Josh. Not her quiet brother, you know, the one who   fucked up that kid at the museum. Not him.

Ava comes in. Josh stands up, and pulls some cash from his pocket.

JOSH   Hey, can you put this with the rest.

AVA   Of course, where'd you get this?

JOSH   Just painted some old man's fence up near Augustine's.

AVA   Oh nice. No luck elsewhere?

Josh shakes his head.

AVA	Look Josh, you know we need to talk about this. Is it not maybe time that you start looking at somewhere else? Somewhere with work? You can't afford to stay here.
JOSH	Nor could you if I left.
AVA	Josh we can't as it is.
JOSH	So what would you do then? If I left Swell tonight?
AVA	Rent a spare room, I guess. Or stay in Elaine's –
JOSH	Elaine's? What kind of life is that, living in a B&B? Is that how you get repaid for all you've done here? Look, let me get one thing straight: I'm not leaving you, Ava. I can't. Where would I go? You're all I've got.

Pause.

JOSH	Come with me though.
AVA	I can't.
JOSH	We could find somewhere else, a new home. As a team.
AVA	Josh, I can't. I'm needed here.
JOSH	So you won't leave 'cause of her? She can find someone else.
AVA	They'll just put her in a home.
JOSH	And what about going back to college?
AVA	What about it?
JOSH	What do you mean? You had plans, Ava. You still have your life to live.
AVA	Life gets in the way.
JOSH	Nah, it doesn't have to be like that. You've given so much to this place, this community –
AVA	Look, this romanticism is fine but right now the cold facts are we're a couple hundred short for the month. And we're running out of time.
JOSH	Can't they give us a bit longer? I can do a couple more jobs, we can get the money –

AVA   They've already given us extensions, for the past four months. They know we're on a single income now. We're out of favours.

JOSH   What about Marlowe? Can she not help at all?

AVA   She has helped, Josh, more than anyone. She's given me a job, cashflow.

JOSH   It's not enough.

AVA   Look Josh, I really appreciate everything you've done for me. I do. You've stayed here when you didn't have to, and you've paid for it as much as anyone else. But at some point, we have to admit when our time's up.

Ava exits and Josh is left alone on stage. Tense.

JOSH   In my head there's this pressure. Like a hydraulic press squeezing a can tighter and tighter. Not a minute of clarity. One thought leading into the next leading into the next before the one before's even finished, ideas spinning around my head like post-it notes thrown into a storm. All I can see in some vague certainty is Ava. Ava, who has rescued me time after time after time but who I can never help when it's my time to be there. Ava, who for all my life I've envied as much as I've loved. Who has dedicates her life to these people. A town on the edge but instead of holding each other tighter we push and we push so that we're not the ones hanging over the side. And then I see Adi, and my mind, fucked on regret and frustration takes me to some place I could have been if I had said yes to him. Somewhere I could still be, somewhere where I could fix this all if I just had more time.
And as if I'm on driftwood down a white-water stream, I see protestors against wire gates, dropping soft toys into buckets and clapping and cheering as we clutched our redundancy packages beneath our arms and where are they now? Where are their witty one liners and rain dances now it's our lives? Human lives? Not some fucking abstract, not a prediction or a theory, this is real fucking life. Where are the visitors who said Swell was their best kept secret, until their secret started to chip and crack and instead of help, they scattered?

Seaweed and David confront me, Andy too. My mistakes.
Impulsive, stupid, dumb decisions, so easy to make, so hard to
make right. And my dad, who taught me to always to be the
best man I can be, is disappointed in me. But he can't be
disappointed because he's in the dirt. And he'd help me find a
way out but he won't find the way out with me because he's in
the dirt. And he'd see what's happening in our home and he'd
bring people together and we'd get through it and he'd help
like Ava, because Ava's just like him, but he can't see what's
happening and he can't bring people together because he's in
the fucking dirt. Because he'll never get old on a foldable chair
in front of a beach hut moaning at rowdy schoolkids because
for him he's still in that fucking doorway gripping, ripping at
his chest.

And Mrs Marlowe. Mrs Marlowe, who's given Ava a job. Mrs
Marlowe, who's put money in our pockets and food on our
table but not enough keep this roof over our heads. Mrs
Marlowe, who once owned half of Swell, who sleeps on a
mattress of bullseyes, who Ava won't now leave Swell because
of but at the same time because of her can't afford to stay. And
she could help! She could pay my sister better or give her a
loan or <u>something.</u> She's the selfishness of this town.

These post-it note thoughts cover me like a fucking swarm
until... clarity.

Act Three

Josh puts on a hoodie, and creeps out of his flat.

JOSH   There's no wind tonight. Street's dead. Nothing except for me
and the humming of the streetlights. Down the road, number
166. Front garden choked by weeds, wood chipped front door
locked, tattered white curtains drawn. Clarity.

I duck around the side of the house, mouth dry, heartbeat

pounding in my ears. Back terrace swamped too. A singular gnome sits with his fishing rod, staring at me. Like he's seeing me. And he's got this grin. This stupid grin. Laughing at me, hood up and down low, like I'm some fucking criminal. Prick. I lift him up, grab the key.

Josh puts the key in the back door and – click. It opens.

JOSH   Belly of the beast. As my eyes adjust to the dark the room comes into focus. A living room. I press forward, carpet silencing my approach. Down the hall a door ajar, a raspy breathing within.

Josh opens the door. It creaks quietly.

JOSH   A body lies still under blankets, and across the room – (*He jumps*) My silver bullets. Before I know it I'm there. On the desk are necklaces, rings, bracelets, brooches. I take them, slowly, quietly, almost numb to my own hands moving from desk to bag like I've done this a million times. A small box sits to the side, and when I've got more than I need I find myself then needing more. I open it slowly, and inside I think there's –

Delicate music plays from the music box. Josh closes it quickly, with a slam.

JOSH   Shit!

He pauses.

JOSH   A groaning beneath the blankets. I reach for my bag... Slowly...
MRS M Who's that? My Ralph?
JOSH   Back against the black, I will myself to dart it from the darkness but my feet won't move. She sits up, heavy from her slumber, eyes adjusting to the room she knows so well. Eyes lock with clouded grey pupils. Not her Ralph. Not even close. And my feet, still nailed to this spot. Her eyes widen, her

mouth parts and it looks like she's screaming but just a raspy gurgle finds air. She tries to push herself away from this shadow in the black but her strength abandons her. And she starts grabbing at her chest. She's ripping, gripping at her night gown. And suddenly my feet release me.

Without a second's rest I bolt it. Slam into the hallway, photo frames smash to the floor. Living room races past me, back door thrown open, gnome kicked across the garden and meets the fence with a smash. No longer bent low, I'm back over the fence, sprint down the street exposed under the street lights, wrestle my front door open and –

FUCK! FUCK!! FUCK FUCK FUCK FUCK! FUCK! FUCK!

Ava enters in a dressing gown, woken by the noise.

AVA   Josh? What's happened?

JOSH   Ava... I've really messed up this time, Ava.

AVA   (*Scared*) What do you mean? What have you done?

Josh slides the rucksack over. She opens it, pulling the jewellery out.

AVA   This is... Josh... No.

JOSH   She woke up. I woke her up when I was there and she saw me. She got spooked, she started panicking. And then she... I couldn't do anything.

The colour drains from Ava's face. She steadies herself.

JOSH   I wanted to help. I couldn't leave you, you're the only thing I have left. I've got nothing if I don't have you, Ava.

AVA   Josh, why?

JOSH   Why?

AVA   Yes, why? What were you thinking?

JOSH   Well... We need money, to stay. We needed more time. I thought... Well, I thought I could- I was going to sell it. If I had more time I would've been able to –

AVA   You robbed her whilst she slept?

JOSH   I wasn't stealing. I was going to give it back, I swear.

AVA   You just said you were going to sell it.

JOSH   I was going to buy it back! I just needed the money to keep us here, and then I was going to sort everything out. I was going to step up, I can't keep fucking things –

AVA   And what have you done now, Josh?! She's dead, is that what you're telling me?

Josh nods solemnly.

AVA   What exactly do you think I'm supposed to do here now?

JOSH   What do you mean?

AVA   Josh, you've killed someone – what are you not understanding?

JOSH   But I didn't mean to –

AVA   Manslaughter, third degree, whatever you want to fucking call it – do you not get it?

JOSH   But they won't... Maybe they won't know –

AVA   How will they not know? All her jewellery is gone and she's –

JOSH   I'll return it. I could go now –

AVA   I know, Josh! Do you not get it? I know.

JOSH   You can't tell them –

AVA   Every single decision I've made in my life has been for us. For me and you. Every single one. And what's that all been for?

JOSH   That's not fair –

AVA   Every fucking decision! And every time you throw that in my face, every time you do something so mind-numbingly stupid,

I think to myself this will be his time to learn. This will be the moment he grows up. What did I do wrong, Josh? What did I get so disastrously wrong in the past five years that led us here?

JOSH   Ava, you were perfect.

AVA   So then it's not my fault at all? I have no responsibility. And all those nights I've stayed up feeling sick trying to keep us with some sort of security, that was all pointless, was it? Because no matter how good a job I did, you were still going to end up breaking and entering –

JOSH   No. No that's not what I... Ava it's not my fault, I didn't –

AVA   Of course it's your fault Josh! This position we're in was put onto us. But everything else, you had a choice. You always have a choice, Josh.

Pause.

AVA   You need to go.

JOSH   What?

AVA   You need to go, now.

JOSH   Go where?

AVA   I don't know, Josh, I don't want to know because if I know I'll have to tell them, but you need to get your shit together, right now, and get the fuck out of Swell. I'll keep quiet until the morning and then I have to tell them what I know.

JOSH   Ava, please. I swear I can make this right –

AVA   I can't protect you from this one Josh! Go!

Josh tries to say something, but the words won't come. He turns around, and runs. Ava is left alone on stage.

AVA   I wait on her front step as the ambulance arrives. The night's cold, but there's no wind. A swift study of her frail figure finds her dead upon arrival. Heart attack. A quick but agonizing ecstasy in the embrace of her blankets. Died in her own bed, everyone's dream, right?

Sleep is an abstract tonight. An unintelligible assault of moments. At some point in this endless stretch, my feet take me from the apartment, and towards the heart of Swell. Beating barely, unaware it's about to be broken in half by this terrible tragedy. I walk onto the high street. Past wooden boards and chipped plaster and the acrylic violations of bored, desultory drones on the beach huts.

This place, this best kept secret, God's garden. Our placative public profile was our draw. Sleepy old Hamelin, too polite to chase the piper as he pulled their community apart.

But this world was fractured since before the meeting when we packed inside St Augustine's like lamb fat for the slaughter. It cracked when dad left us. It continued to splinter and now Josh has gone too. And Adi, and Dawn, and anyone else who was lucky enough to pull themselves out. And now, what's left? A smashed reflection, some semblance of a place from my memories but none of those images quite right. A legacy built on sandcastles, washed away as quick as it was created.

And as the sea draws in, it laughs. It's permanence a perpetual reminder of what we fall for. And yet still, it dances back and forth like a heartbeat, steady, never breaching its routine to reclaim the town. Not once in over twenty years, and not once since the yellow tape and the small print. It pulls in, in, in, and out.

As orange streaks against red and purple turns to blue, as bubbles froth in the pebbled cracks of the shore and the gulls begin to glide, as the streetlamps flicker off and the sun rises through the ocean, I lie here, in this spot where we toasted Dad's birthday. In this spot where he once lay, catching his breath whilst clutching our treasure on his soaking chest. In this spot where I have watched countless sunrises and countless sunsets. And I realise we were foolish to ever call this place our own.

She breaths in. As she breaths out, we hear the sound of the tide breaking against the shore instead. The lights dim. We hear the ocean.

THE END.

Printed in Great Britain
by Amazon